Happy 4th of July, Jenny Sweeney!

Leslie Kimmelman

Illustrated by Nancy Cote

Albert Whitman & Company • Morton Grove, Illinois

To my dad, who taught me
everything I know about
flag etiquette, press conferences,
and the music of John Philip Sousa.
—L. K.

For all the children touched
by the events of 9/11.
—N. C.

Library of Congress Cataloging-in-Publication Data
Kimmelman, Leslie.
Happy 4th of July, Jenny Sweeney! /
by Leslie Kimmelman ; illustrated by Nancy Cote.
p. cm.
Summary: Town residents prepare to celebrate the
Fourth of July with food, a parade, and fireworks.
ISBN 0-8075-3152-9 (hardcover)
[1. Fourth of July—Fiction. 2. Stories in rhyme.] I. Cote, Nancy, ill.
II. Title. PZ8.3.K5598 Hap 2003 [E]—dc21 2002011327

Text copyright © 2003 by Leslie Kimmelman.
Illustrations copyright © 2003 by Nancy Cote.
Published in 2003 by Albert Whitman & Company,
6340 Oakton Street, Morton Grove, Illinois 60053-2723.
www.albertwhitman.com.
10 9 8 7 6 5 4 3 2

The design is by Carol Gildar.

For more information about Albert Whitman & Company,
visit our web site at www.albertwhitman.com.

Sun's up high,
Fourth of July!
Lots of preparation
for a day of celebration.

Jenny Sweeney washes Rags.

Mrs. Berger hangs up flags.

Fireman Mike scrubs down his truck.

Quentin has beginner's luck.

The Dalal family smiles proudly.
"We're Americans now!" they proclaim loudly.

Arjun dashes through the spray.
That rascal Rags—he runs away!

Lisa practices her twirling.

Luis salutes the flag unfurling.

Mr. Jonas finds his cap.

Baby Lily takes a nap.

Mayor Swanson writes her speech.

Rags keeps running
out of reach!

Mr. Hill fires up the grill.
All the family eats their fill.

Katie toots her piccolo.

Jenny ties a big red bow.

Emma finishes her float:

"Uncle Sam Wants You to Vote!"

Mayor Swanson tests the mike.
Jenny's ready on her bike.

Jimmy Yang sips lemonade.
Look! It's time for the parade!

Let the celebration start!
Everybody plays a part.

Gladly, proudly, down the street,

joyful music, marching feet.

Fireworks light up the dark
as Jenny watches in the park.

What a party!
What a day—

Happy Birthday, U.S.A.!

About America's Birth

July 4, 1776, was the day the United States of America was born. On that day, a congress of the colonies adopted the Declaration of Independence, proclaiming America's freedom from Great Britain. The Declaration begins: "We hold these truths to be self-evident, that all men are created equal . . ."

Celebrations started a few days later and continued for many days. With no cars or telephones, information traveled slowly, so it took a while for everyone to hear the news. Americans celebrated much the way we do today, with picnics, fireworks, and parades. The first actual celebrations on July 4th itself took place the next year, in July 1777.

★ The first American flag had thirteen stars and thirteen stripes, one star and one stripe for each of the original thirteen colonies. At first the idea was to add a new star and stripe for every new state. After Vermont and Kentucky joined the nation in 1791 and 1792, the American flag had fifteen stars and fifteen stripes—and the country was growing. So in 1818, Congress set the number of stripes back to thirteen with one star for each state. Today's flag has fifty stars but just thirteen stripes. Can you imagine how big a fifty-stripe flag would have to be?

★ Do you know what the national bird is? A bald eagle. Benjamin Franklin wanted it to be a wild turkey!

★ On July 4, 1826, America's fiftieth birthday, former president John Adams and former president Thomas Jefferson died within hours of each other. Jefferson had written the Declaration of Independence, and John Adams had played a leading role in the Declaration's adoption. In 1831, former president James Monroe also died on July 4th. On July 4, 1872, Calvin Coolidge was born. He would one day be the thirtieth president of the United States.

★ The Liberty Bell was made many years before the United States became a nation. It can still be seen hanging in Liberty Bell Pavilion, near Independence Hall in Philadelphia. Engraved on its side are words from the Bible: "Proclaim liberty throughout the land unto all the inhabitants thereof." On July 4, 1776, the Liberty Bell was rung to call citizens to the first public reading of the Declaration of Independence. Because it has a large crack, the bell hasn't been rung since 1846.